S0-CVH-740

Animal Diaries
Life Cycles

A Periodical Cicada's Life

by
Ellen Lawrence

Consultant:

Gregory Hoover
Ornamental Entomologist, Department of Entomology
Pennsylvania State University
University Park, Pennsylvania

New York, New York

Credits

Cover, © Steve Byland/Shutterstock; TOC, © Daniel Dempster Photography/Alamy; 4, © Lopolo/Shutterstock; 5, © B. Mete Uz/Alamy; 6, © Martin Shields/Alamy; 7, © Mitsuhiko Imamori/Minden Pictures/FLPA; 8, © Clarence Holmes Wildlife/Alamy; 9, © Clarence Holmes Wildlife/Alamy; 10, © Animals/Animals/Superstock; 11, © Doug Wechsler/Nature Picture Library; 11R, © Doug Wechsler; 12, © Daniel Dempster Photography/Alamy; 13, © Enigma/Alamy; 14, © Grant Heilman Photography/Alamy; 15, © Andrew Skolnick/Shutterstock; 16, © Clarence Holmes Wildlife/Alamy; 17, © Macroscopic Solutions, LLC. www.macroscopicsolutions.com; 18R, © Lev Savitskiy/Shutterstock; 18–19, © Animals/Animals/Superstock; 20, © Lopolo/Shutterstock; 21, © Steve Byland/IstockPhoto; 22T, © Andrew Skolnick/Shutterstock; 22C, © Macroscopic Solutions, LLC. www.macroscopicsolutions.com; 22B, © B. Mete Uz/Alamy; 23TL, © B. Mete Uz/Alamy; 23TC, © Shutterstock; 23TR, © Enigma/Alamy; 23BL, © Martin Shields/Alamy; 23BC, © Doug Wechsler/Nature Picture Library; 23BR, Steve Byland/Shutterstock.

Publisher: Kenn Goin
Senior Editor: Joyce Tavolacci
Creative Director: Spencer Brinker
Design: Emma Randall
Photo Researcher: Ruby Tuesday Books Ltd

Library of Congress Cataloging-in-Publication Data

Names: Lawrence, Ellen, 1967– author.
Title: A periodical cicada's life / by Ellen Lawrence.
Description: New York, New York : Bearport Publishing, [2017] | Series:
    Animal diaries: Life cycles | Audience: Ages 6–10. | Includes
    bibliographical references and index.
Identifiers: LCCN 2016012268 (print) | LCCN 2016015637 (ebook) | ISBN
    9781944102470 (library binding) | ISBN 9781944997403 (ebook)
Subjects: LCSH: Cicadas—Juvenile literature. | Life cycles
    (Biology)—Juvenile literature.
Classification: LCC QL527.C5 L39 2017 (print) | LCC QL527.C5 (ebook) | DDC
    595.7/52—dc23
LC record available at https://lccn.loc.gov/2016012268

For more information, write to Bearport Publishing Company, Inc., 45 West 21st Street, Suite 3B, New York, New York 10010. Printed in the United States of America.

10 9 8 7 6 5 4 3 2 1

Contents

A Big Night in a Forest...............4

Growing Up.........................6

More Amazing Changes 8

Millions of Bugs......................10

Singing Cicadas 12

Time to Lay Eggs 14

Hello, Nymphs!.......................16

Life Underground 18

A Long Time!.........................20

Science Lab 22

Science Words 23

Index 24

Read More 24

Learn More Online 24

About the Author 24

Name: Sophia   **Date:** May 15

A Big Night in a Forest

Just before dark, I visited a forest near my house to see something amazing.

Thousands of wingless brown **insects** were crawling out of the ground.

Dad told me the insects are periodical cicadas (si-KAY-duhs).

At this stage in their life, they are called **nymphs**.

Can you believe the cicada nymphs have been living underground for 17 years?

Millions of nymphs **emerge** from the ground at the same time. How do they know when to do this? It's a mystery that scientists are still trying to solve!

periodical cicada nymph

What do you think the cicada nymphs do after emerging from the ground?

Date: _May 16_____

Growing Up

During the night, the nymphs climbed up trees in the forest.

As each one held tightly onto a tree, its brown skin began to crack.

After about one hour, the insect wriggled out of its skin.

It now has a new yellowish-white body and wings!

Dad says this is the adult stage of the periodical cicada's life.

yellowish-white adult cicada

old, brown nymph skin

After a cicada nymph sheds its skin, the skin eventually falls to the ground. Sometimes the ground is covered with thousands of empty skins!

old nymph skin

adult periodical cicada

Imagine you are describing an adult cicada to a friend who's never seen one. How would you describe it?

More Amazing Changes

It's been a week since I visited the forest, and the cicadas have changed again!

Instead of yellowish-white, their bodies are now black and orange.

Their wings have changed color, too.

Dad says it took less than a day for the cicadas' white bodies to darken.

red eye

tiny eye

Cicadas have two reddish-orange eyes and three tiny eyes. Like all insects, they have six legs and a hard outer skin called an exoskeleton.

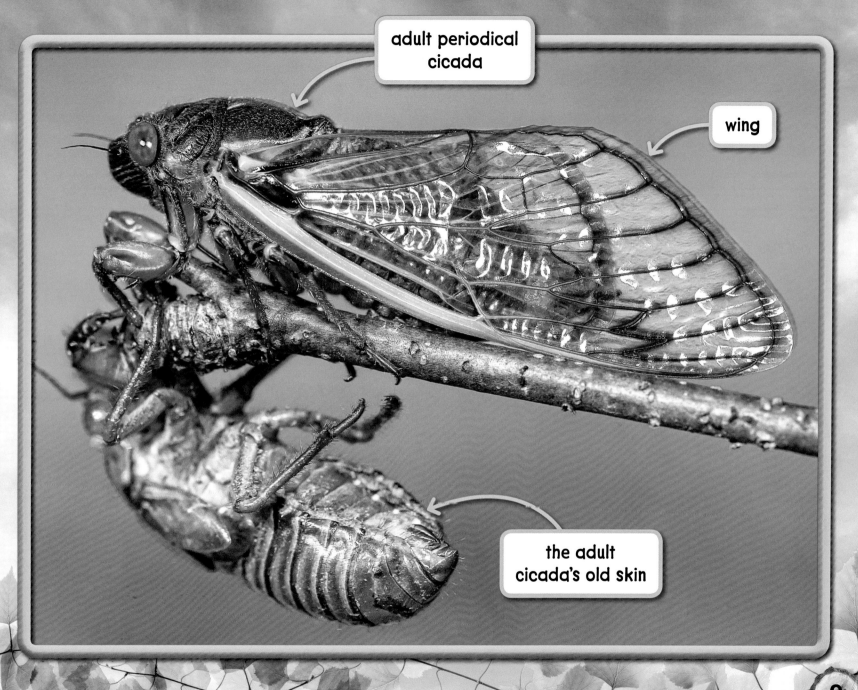

adult periodical cicada

wing

the adult cicada's old skin

Date: _May 24_____

Millions of Bugs

Everywhere I look, **swarms** of cicadas are flying from tree to tree.

I also see birds chasing after the insects.

Robins, starlings, wild turkeys, and other birds catch and eat them.

Dad says squirrels, mice, snakes, and toads feed on them, too!

a toad eating a cicada

a swarm of periodical cicadas on a tree

Cicadas feed on juices called sap that flow through the branches of trees. They suck up the sap through mouthparts that work like a straw.

straw-like mouthparts

When millions of cicadas are in a forest, it gets very noisy. Why do you think this is?

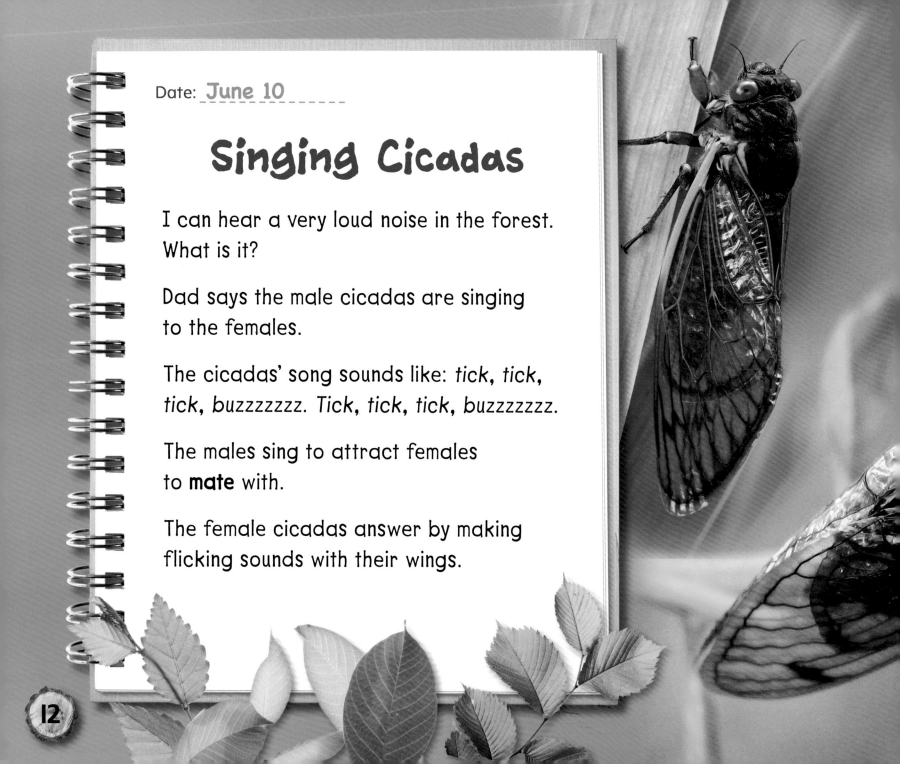

Date: <u>June 10</u>

Singing Cicadas

I can hear a very loud noise in the forest. What is it?

Dad says the male cicadas are singing to the females.

The cicadas' song sounds like: *tick, tick, tick, buzzzzzzz. Tick, tick, tick, buzzzzzzz.*

The males sing to attract females to **mate** with.

The female cicadas answer by making flicking sounds with their wings.

Male cicadas have parts inside their bodies that vibrate like the top of a drum. These parts, called **tymbals**, are used to make the cicadas' song.

Date: June 14

Time to Lay Eggs

A few days after mating, a female cicada lays her eggs on branches and twigs.

Today, Dad and I watched a female making a small cut in the bark of a twig.

She did this using a saw-like part on the end of her body.

Next, she laid 24 tiny white eggs inside the cut.

Then she made more cuts in the twig and laid more eggs.

periodical cicada eggs

A female cicada can lay up to 600 eggs.

a female periodical cicada laying eggs

small cut

saw-like body part

Date: __July 26__

Hello, Nymphs!

It's been six weeks since we watched the female cicada laying her eggs.

We visited the forest today, and it was very quiet.

The adult cicadas have all died.

Dad has something exciting to show me, though.

Millions of tiny white nymphs are hatching from the cicada eggs!

old nymph skins and dead adult cicadas on the forest floor

Adult cicadas only live for about four weeks.

This newly hatched cicada nymph is smaller than a grain of rice.

What do you think the newly hatched cicada nymphs will do next?

Date: July 27

Life Underground

After the nymphs hatch, they fall from the tree branches onto the ground.

Then they use their large front legs to bury themselves in the soil.

In their dark, underground world, the nymphs feed on juices from plant roots.

They suck up the juices with their straw-like mouthparts.

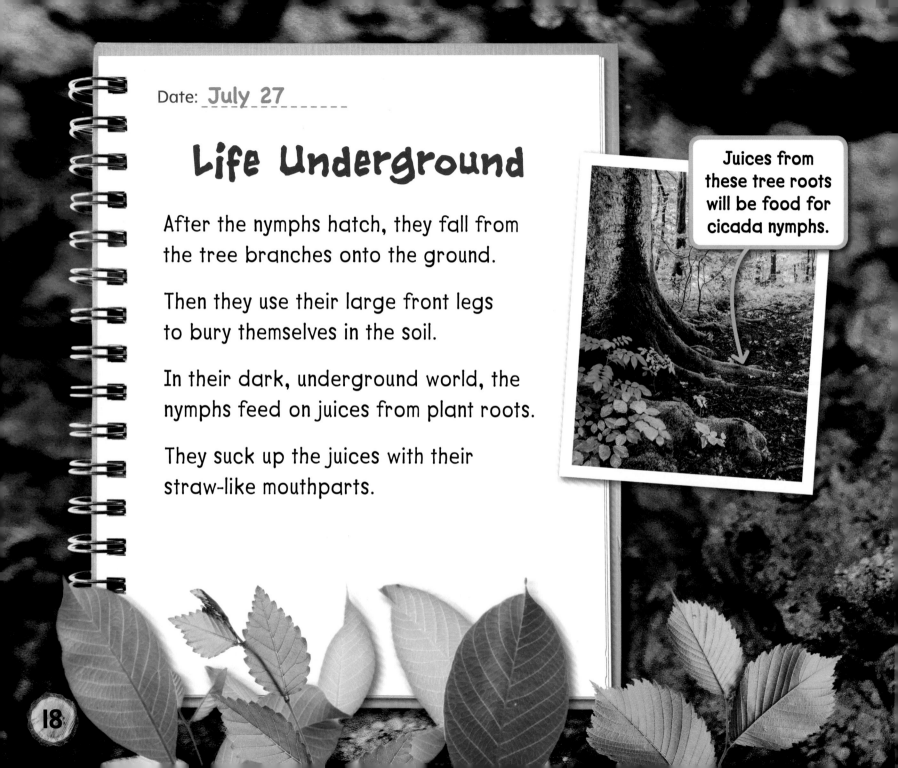

Juices from these tree roots will be food for cicada nymphs.

periodical cicada nymphs
digging in the soil

Cicada
nymphs can live
2 feet (0.6 m) below
the surface of
the ground.

19

Date: <u>August 1</u>

A Long Time!

Today, I went for a walk in the forest.

It's hard to believe there are millions of cicada nymphs living in the soil under my feet.

Dad says the nymphs will grow and change over a very long time.

Then in 17 years, they will crawl out of the ground to begin their adult lives.

The next time I see the cicadas in the forest, I'll be an adult myself!

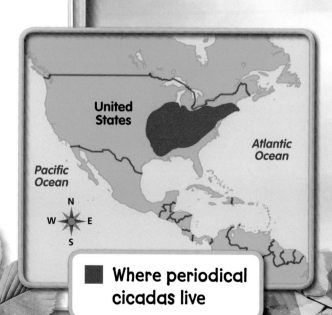

Where periodical cicadas live

Periodical cicadas live longer than any other insect in the United States. Some periodical cicadas have a 17-year life cycle. Others live for 13 years.

a 17-year-old adult cicada

Science Lab

Make a Periodical Cicada Diary

Imagine that you are a scientist studying periodical cicadas.

Write a diary about the insect's life using the information in this book.

Include these life cycle stages in your diary.

- **A female cicada lays eggs.**

- **A nymph hatches from an egg.**

- **A nymph lives underground for 17 years.**

- **The nymph emerges from the soil and changes into an adult cicada.**

Draw pictures to include in your diary, and then present your diary to friends and family.

Read the questions below and think about the answers.

You can include some of the information from your answers in the diary.

Look at the pictures. They will help you, too.

- *Where does a female periodical cicada lay her eggs?*

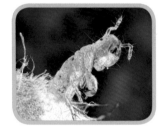

- *What does a newly hatched nymph look like?*

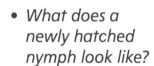

- *What happens to a nymph as it changes into an adult?*

- *Describe an adult cicada in the final stage of its life.*

Science Words

emerge (ih-MURJ) to move out of something and come into view

insects (IN-sekts) small animals that have six legs, three main body parts, two antennae, and a hard covering called an exoskeleton

mate (MAYT) to come together to produce young

nymphs (NIMFS) the young of some insects, such as cicadas and grasshoppers

swarms (SWARMZ) large groups of flying insects that live together

tymbals (TIM-buhls) parts inside insects that vibrate to make noise

Index

birds 10

eggs 14–15, 16, 22

exoskeleton 8

eyes 8

feeding 10–11, 18

mating 12–13, 14

mouthparts 11, 18

nymphs 4–5, 6–7, 9, 16–17, 18–19, 20, 22

singing 12–13

toads 10

trees 6, 10–11, 14, 18

tymbals 13

wings 6, 8–9, 12

Read More

Amstutz, Lisa J. *Cicadas (Creepy Crawlers)*. North Mankato, MN: Capstone (2013).

Hall, Margaret. *Cicadas* (Bugs, Bugs, Bugs!) North Mankato, MN: Capstone (2006).

Roza, Greg. *The Bizarre Life Cycle of a Cicada (Strange Life Cycles)*. New York: Gareth Stevens (2012).

Learn More Online

To learn more about periodical cicadas, visit **www.bearportpublishing.com/AnimalDiaries**

About the Author

Ellen Lawrence lives in the United Kingdom. Her favorite books to write are those about animals. In fact, the first book Ellen bought for herself when she was six years old was the story of a gorilla named Patty Cake that was born in New York's Central Park Zoo.